Pancakes

by Diane G. Silver

illustrated by Bob Doucet

HOUGHTON MIFFLIN HARCOURT
School Publishers

Printed in China

ISBN-13: 978-0-547-01669-6
ISBN-10: 0-547-01669-7

13 14 15 16 0940 19 18 17 16
4500569761

"It is now time to rise, little friend," said a toneless voice. Ari rolled over, rubbed her eyes, and glared at Tempo. "Go away," she mumbled and pulled her bedcovers over her head.

"I cannot go away. It is my responsibility to ensure that you rise in a timely manner," the clockbot responded. "Now please rise immediately."

That's the problem with these bots, Ari thought to herself. *They take their jobs too seriously.* With a sigh that admitted defeat, she threw off the blankets and stood up. "So, what time is it, Tempo?"

"It is now 0600 hours," Tempo responded. "You are expected at school in 44 minutes, 50.5 seconds."

Ari rubbed her eyes again. "Okay," she said, "you've done your job," and began grabbing clothes.

"Good morning, Ari," Grandma Neila called as Ari rushed into the narrow galley. "What are you eating today, my dear?"

"Oh, I don't know… an egg scramble, I guess," Ari replied. She stepped up to the nutrient condenser. "Hi, N.C. One egg scramble, please."

"This tasty, convenient, high-density, high-nutrient pellet is guaranteed to keep you happily fueled for a minimum of seven hours," announced the condenser. Ari heard the clunk of the nickel-sized pellet hitting the bottom of its receptacle. She lifted the acrylic cover, popped the warm, speckled pellet into her mouth, and began chewing.

"Yum!" said the condenser.

Just then, Tempo joined them in the galley. "If you do not leave in two minutes, twelve seconds, you will be late for school," he intoned.

"Time me," said Ari, swallowing the last of her breakfast and bending over to kiss her grandma goodbye. But Grandma didn't offer her cheek. Ari suddenly noticed that she was staring off into the distance. "Grandma," she asked with a touch of worry, "are you feeling all right? You haven't touched your oatmeal pellet."

"Oh, no, I'm fine, dear. I was just thinking about my own grandma, and what a wonderful *cook* she was. When I was a little girl, she would rustle up stacks of pancakes for Sunday morning breakfast. How delicious they were! They smelled like a spice tray and tasted like buttery clouds! I know it makes me sound ancient to say it, but I do miss real food sometimes—especially pancakes."

"What are pancakes?" asked Ari.

But before Grandma Neila could reply, Tempo began chanting: "10... 9... 8..." Ari gave her grandmother a hasty kiss and rushed away. "Sorry, Grandma," she called over her shoulder. "Gotta fly. See you later!"

Piloting her Personal Air Vehicle at the maximum allowable speed for a junior operator, Ari made it to class with eight seconds to spare. That morning, though, she found it uncharacteristically difficult to concentrate. In her mind, she kept replaying the description of her great-great-grandmother's Sunday morning pancakes. Ari decided she needed to find out more about pancakes. And she felt hungry. She decided that the condenser was definitely wrong about staying happily fueled for seven hours.

At noon, Ari caught up with her friends Leda and Drey on the way to the school pelleteria. "I'm ready for nutrients," Drey was saying. "Come on, let's get burrito pellets." The trio headed toward the wall of nutrient condensers. As she stepped around a clump of kids, Ari collided head-on with a boy.

"Sorry," she said with some embarrassment. "I didn't see you coming."

"No harm, no foul. I'm fine," he responded and kept walking.

"Who's that?" Ari asked after he was gone. "I don't recognize him."

"His name is Nikko," said Drey as she slowly chewed her burrito pellet. "I heard a rumor that his family came here from the Hinterlands."

"People there are so backward!" Leda sniffed. "Some don't even use smart-helper robots. What's up with…"

"Hey, have you ever heard of pancakes?" Ari interrupted. "My grandmother was talking about them this morning. They're some kind of food people cooked in the old days. Grandma says they taste like buttery clouds."

Leda shrugged. "Why would you want to know about some old *food?* The high-density, high-nutrient pellets we get from condensers are tasty and convenient."

"So say the robots," Ari said, a bit sarcastically.

"There are some people in the Hinterlands who still cook," Drey said.

"That's so weird!" declared Leda. "Pellets are easy and quick. We don't waste time preparing meals and then sitting around eating them. Those yokels should get a modern life!"

The school clockbot ended the discussion with its call to classes.

After school, Ari flew straight home and headed to her grandma's alcove. "Grandma, tell me more about the food you called pancakes. I can't get your description out of my mind!"

"What can I say?" Grandma sighed. "Fluffy, golden-brown pancakes were one of my favorite foods when I was growing up."

"How do you make them?" asked Ari.

"Unfortunately, I don't really know," Grandma told her. "I was just five years old when my grandma passed away. That's when the family stopped cooking. We did what everyone else was doing—we got rid of our stove, refrigerator, pots, plates, and silverware, and leased a nutrient condenser. The pellets were so tasty and convenient! We threw away our recipes, too."

Grandma Neila paused, and her tone of voice changed. "Now I wonder why we did that. Even if we weren't going to use them, we should have kept them for the memories."

As Grandma spoke, a plan started brewing in Ari's mind. "Recipes," Ari said. "I've heard of them. And I think I know where to find them…"

The two humans were not the only ones interested in the conversation. A smart-helper robot was listening in. The talk about homemade food set off alarms inside the nutrient condenser. Its collective memory chip flashed an internal alert:

```
Noncondensed food can have a dangerous
hypnotic effect on people and change
their behavior in impractical ways, even
bringing back primitive practices like
sitting down with family members and
eating long, leisurely meals together.
```

The nutrient condenser had deduced that Ari was plotting to prepare real food—pancakes, to be specific.

```
Cooking impulses are counterproductive
and dangerous. The family could develop
a taste for real food and fail to renew
my lease.
```

The condenser's circuits glowed with stress. It would have felt desperate if it had been human.

The next morning, Tempo's sensors got quite a shock. Ari was already out of bed and dressed. The slightly confused clockbot followed her into the galley—ready to urge, to chide, to count down—but he found it hard to be his collected robotic self when Ari was so many minutes ahead of schedule.

"My goodness, you're up bright and early today. I'm impressed!" Grandma Neila said as Ari bounded up and gave her a hug.

"Salutations, Ari!" the nutrient condenser announced, a little too loudly. "What universally-enjoyed flavor of nourishing fuel may I condense for you this morning?"

"Hey, N.C., no pellets right now," Ari said. "I'll just grab a sustenance cracker. I gotta get to school early." She kissed Grandma and ran out the portal to her PAV.

As soon as she landed on the school flight deck, Ari was off to the HoloLab. She plunked herself down at a terminal and said, "Ari Herald logging in."

"Good morning, Ari," the HoloGuide responded. "How may I help you today?"

"First, I need to know all about pancakes, and second, I need a real, old-fashioned recipe that explains how to cook them."

"Holographic research is commencing—now locating 'pancakes,' ancient culinary history."

Before Ari could say thank you, a holographic stack of pancakes floated tantalizingly toward her, and she could smell a toasty, buttery, holographically generated smell in the air.

A definition appeared just underneath the stack of pancakes. It read, "Pancakes: a disc-shaped, grain-based foodstuff widely consumed until the end of the 21st century; pancakes were usually cooked in a frying pan (see Frying Pan)."

Then a shower of holographic recipes began whirling around Ari's head. "Too many to choose from!" she exclaimed. "How on earth do I know which one to pick?"

Just then, Ari felt someone tap the back of her chair. She turned around and saw Nikko, the transfer student. He said, "Hi, Ari. I saw your floating pancakes. Have you ever tried them?"

"Have you?" Ari blurted out. "I mean, well, I'm a little curious about them—even though they aren't exactly convenient."

"Well," Nikko explained, "back where I come from, some people still cook them. In fact, quite a few of us still cook all kinds of food the old-fashioned way—and my Uncle Robertus makes the best pancakes of anyone I know. Mom and I are going to visit him this Saturday. Ask if you can come with us. Uncle Robertus can show you how to make real golden pancakes."

"Wow! That's so nice of you," Ari said, relieved. "I was feeling kind of overwhelmed by the recipes. It'll be so much easier to learn from a person! But I'm not sure my grandma will let me go to such a primitive—"

Ari stopped, horrified by the statement she had thoughtlessly begun.

"If your grandma told you about pancakes, she's wise enough to know that there's nothing wrong with being a little old-fashioned," Nikko said.

As it turned out, Nikko's family wasn't entirely old-fashioned. Their PAV made the 3,000-mile journey to their Hinterlands destination in less than an hour. The sun was barely above the horizon when Ari, Nikko, and his mom walked into an odd-looking dwelling made of wood.

They found Uncle Robertus bustling around a room different from any Ari had ever seen. "This is a *kitchen*," Nikko explained. "It's a room used for preparing and storing food."

"I've heard of kitchens," Ari said, "but I didn't know they looked like this."

Shelves, boxes, and counters ran around the edges of the room. Uncle Robertus pointed out a tall, humming box he called a *fridge* that kept food cold. He explained that, unlike condensed nutrient pellets, old-fashioned food could "go bad" if it wasn't cooked promptly or stored properly. Then he showed her a large cooking device called a *stove*. Ari also marveled at the array of tools Uncle Robertus took from the drawers. And then "Chef Robertus," as Nikko's mom called him, went to work.

He whisked together some pale, grainy substances in a large bowl. Then he mixed in two yellowish liquids and a white one. One of the yellow ones looked thick and slimy. Using a big spoon, he stirred the contents of the bowl until they became a gooey mixture. "That's pancake batter," Nikko told the spellbound Ari.

Next Uncle Robertus produced something called a *frying pan* and placed it on the stove. Ari remembered that the holographic definition had mentioned this device. "First we have to heat the surface of the pan," Uncle Robertus explained. "Then we can cook the batter."

Uncle Robertus then did a remarkable thing. Using a large spoon called a *ladle*, he poured big, drippy scoops of the batter into the frying pan. The thick goo sizzled and spluttered when it touched the pan. Ari jumped back, shocked by the noise. "Are you sure this is safe?" she cried.

Nikko and Uncle Robertus burst into laughter. "Come back, Ari," Nikko's mom said kindly. "Those sounds mean that the pancakes are cooking. In a minute or two, they will be ready to be flipped and cooked on the other side. Watch!"

As if on cue, Uncle Robertus flipped one of the half-fried pancakes. It turned over gracefully and landed wet side down in the pan. Then he handed the spatula to Ari.

"Go on, try it," Nikko urged.

Ari knew she was in trouble as soon as she began to pry the pancake from the pan. She looked like a contortionist as she unsuccessfully tried to balance it on the spatula's slick surface. The round disk landed wet side down on her boot.

"Don't feel bad," Uncle Robertus told her. "It happens to everyone at first."

"It's not as easy as it looks!" Ari said, handing the spatula to Nikko. Nikko's flip wasn't pretty, but at least the pancake landed in the pan. As Ari inhaled the buttery aroma, she noticed something else strange happening. It was her mouth—it was watering!

One bite of Uncle Robertus's pancakes was all Ari needed to understand what Grandma had been talking about. They were golden and toasty on the outside and warm, fluffy, and light as air on the inside. Nikko showed Ari how to pour melted butter and a delectable, honey-colored sauce called *maple syrup* over them.

"These pancakes are incredible," Ari told Uncle Robertus. "I never knew anything could taste so good! Thank you for opening my eyes... nose... mouth... and especially for showing me how to make them!"

"What a nice compliment!" Uncle Robertus said. "And since you can't get pancake ingredients or cooking equipment easily where you live, I'll lend you some." He and Nikko packed up ingredients; a bowl, spatula, and whisk; and a frying pan.

"Now you can surprise your Grandma," Nikko said, handing her a piece of paper. "Here's Uncle Robertus's original recipe."

"You'll also need this," Uncle Robertus said, and gave her a small stove—the kind people once used while engaging in an activity called *camping*. "It's easy to use," Nikko added, and he showed Ari how to turn the burners on and off.

As Ari, Nikko, and Nikko's mom approached the family PAV, Uncle Robertus came dashing toward them. "Wait, I forgot to give you this," he panted and handed Ari her very own ladle.

Ari returned home with a single goal in her mind—to share the wonder of pancakes. The upcoming Monday holiday would provide the perfect opportunity.

Late Sunday, Ari persuaded Leda and Drey to come over for an early morning study session the next day. She invited Nikko, too. She told Grandma Neila to expect a surprise but asked her not to rise too early. And she told Tempo to wake her at 0500 hours, which he did, even though—as he pointed out—it wasn't a school day.

By seven o'clock, Ari had laid out her equipment in the galley and set up her stove. She felt an element of suspense. This would be her first time ever cooking food. As she began opening ingredients, she heard a familiar voice.

"Good morning, Ari. I'm concerned about your health," the nutrient condenser said. "Last week you ate only half the recommended amount of high-density, high-nutrient pellets. The latest research shows that food pellets are highly effective in the fight against malnutrition."

"Oh, hi, N.C.," Ari said distractedly as she continued with her preparations. "Yes, I'm, uh, no—I'm fine. No pellet this morning."

The yellow liquid's jar was hard to open... and then, as Ari used all her strength, the lid suddenly turned. The bottle slid from her hand, and some of the slippery contents spilled on the floor. Ari stepped in it as she moved to grab a towel and suddenly found herself on the floor—covered with flour from the open box she'd hit as she fell.

"Ari, you're discovering what you should have learned in school—real food is hazardous," N.C. continued. "There's danger from germs. Possible vitamin deficiencies. Problems with allergies. Scrapes. Sprains. Not to mention fire danger, if you try to cook."

Ari was barely back on her feet when she heard a beep from the portal. She saw that it was Nikko and buzzed him in.

"I decided to come early in case you needed a little help," he said, smiling at his flour-covered friend.

"Good timing," she replied. "How about wiping the galley floor while I go clean up?"

"Ari, I'd like a word with you," said the nutrient condenser with a worried look.

"What is it now?" Ari replied testily.

"You know, Ari, that the great majority of normal people now use high-density pellets to meet all their daily nutritional needs. Do you really want to be so different from all your friends and neighbors?"

"Look, N.C.," Ari said crossly. "I don't mean to be rude, but you're a service-provider robot. You're not supposed to speak unless spoken to, much less try to pressure me."

"As a smart-helper robot, it's my responsibility to speak out when a crisis is developing."

"It's a crisis when someone doesn't eat pellets for every meal?" queried Nikko skeptically.

"Oh, wait!" Ari exclaimed. "Now I get it. N.C., you're worried that Grandma and I will start eating real food and get rid of you."

The bot did not respond.

"You can relax," Ari said comfortingly. "Our lives are too fast-paced to give up pellets totally. After all, they are so tasty and convenient." She winked at Nikko, who grinned at the last comment.

"So here's how you can help, N.C.," Ari continued. "Please give me a high-density maple sugar pellet."

"That's right! Uncle Robertus forgot to give you syrup!" Nikko exclaimed.

"Well, it's not exactly well-balanced nutrition," N.C. said. "But I guess that's OK once in a while."

"That's one smart bot," Nikko said with a smile.

When Grandma Neila came into the galley 20 minutes later, she was wearing a smile as wide as anything Ari had ever seen. "I'd almost forgotten how irresistible the aromas of maple syrup and frying pancakes are! This is the treat of a lifetime, dear!" And she gave Ari a huge hug.

When Leda and Drey arrived, they were quite happy to learn that the study session would be all about eating—though it took skittish Leda some time to try her first pancake. Both friends agreed that "buttery clouds" was an excellent description of the golden discs.

Then Nikko tried to teach Leda and Drey his pancake-flipping technique, with hilarious results. On Drey's first try, she put a pancake on the ceiling, and then Leda managed to plop one onto her new backpack—wet side down.

The wonderful lingering tastes and smells did not keep the friends from complaining about doing dishes. "Now I see why pellets were invented!" groaned Ari as she scrubbed away at the frying pan.

"I'm always here for you, Ari," said the condenser.

"In that case, N.C., how about being here for me at the sink and finishing up the dishes?"

Everyone laughed, and even the condenser seemed to smile at Ari's request.

Responding

✔ **TARGET SKILL** **Story Structure** What is the conflict that must be resolved in *Pancakes*? What are the important events? What is the resolution? Copy and complete the chart below.

Conflict	Events
?	• ? • Nikko and his Uncle Robertus show Ari how to make real pancakes. • ?
Resolution ?	

✏ Write About It

Text to World Ari learns the almost-forgotten art of cooking real food. Think of another skill that most people no longer know how to do. Write several paragraphs describing this skill.

✔ **TARGET SKILL** **Story Structure** Examine details about characters, setting, and plot.

✔ **TARGET STRATEGY** **Infer/Predict** Use text clues to figure out what the author means or what might happen in the future.

GENRE **Science Fiction** is a fantasy story whose plot often depends on scientific ideas.